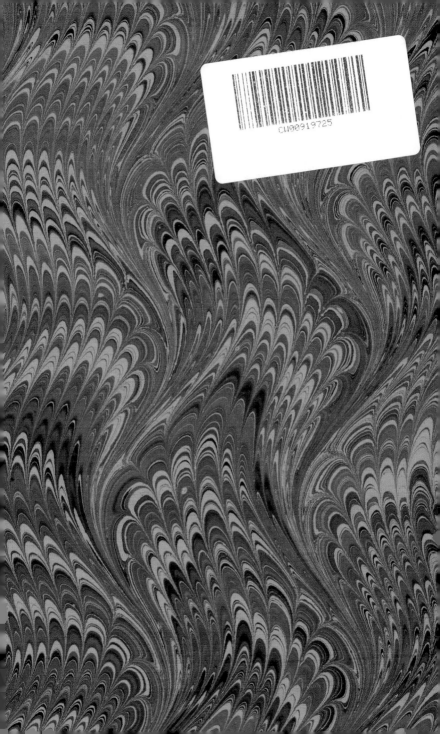

CLASSIC TAILS

The Great Catsby

ELIZA GARRETT

Illustrated by Martin Hargreaves

WILDFIRE

My family, the Cattaways, have been well-to-do felines in the Middle West for generations. But after the Great War I became restless, and I came East – permanently, I thought – in the spring of 'twenty-two.

Across the bay from the less fashionable West Fish, Long Island, where I lived, the white palaces of East Fish glittered along the water. The history of that fateful summer really begins on the evening I drove over there to have din-dins with the wealthy Buchattans. Daisy was my beautiful second cousin, and I'd known Tomcat in college. Really, I scarcely knew them at all.

When I arrived at their elaborate mansion, Tomcat was waiting on the front porch, wearing riding clothes that did not hide the enormous ginger power of his cruel body. 'I've got a nice place here,' he meowed gruffly on my approach.

Inside, two females (one of whom had an unfamiliar scent) were stretched out on a divan. As I came in, Daisy sneezed charmingly and reached for my paw. 'Nick Cattaway! I'm paralysed with happiness!' she cried. She introduced me to Miss Jordan Baker, who yawned and appraised me.

'You live in West Fish,' Jordan sighed contemptuously. 'Why, then, you must know Catsby.'

'Catsby?' demanded Daisy, suddenly serious. 'What Catsby?'

Before I could reply that he was my neighbour, the telephone rang and Tomcat went to answer it. Daisy followed swiftly after a few moments.

I looked with confusion at Jordan, who was trying to listen in. 'Tomcat's got a kitty in the city,' she purred conspiratorially.

Before I'd grasped her meaning there was the swish of a tail, and Daisy and Tomcat were back. 'Couldn't be helped!' my cousin cried with tense gaiety.

After arriving back at my house that night I sat awhile in the yard, and saw I was not alone. Mr Catsby was fifty feet away, gazing out toward the dark water. He stretched out his paws, and though I looked I could see nothing across the bay but two green lights far away, like flashing cats' eyes, at the end of another dock.

When I looked once more for Catsby he had vanished, and I was alone again in the unquiet darkness.

One afternoon I went up to Mew York with Tomcat on the train. About halfway there we stopped in some desolate grey area of land called the valley of ashes, where Tomcat literally forced me from the carriage and said, 'We're getting off. I want you to meet my Myrtle.'

He dragged me to a car garage owned by an anaemic, spiritless mouse called George Wilson, and there we were greeted by Wilson's smouldering mate, Myrtle. 'I want to see you,' hissed Tomcat intently. 'Get on the next train.'

So Tomcat Buchattan and his kitty and I went up together to Mew York.

We went to the small apartment
Tomcat kept in the city, and he
brought out a couple of bottles of milk; I
have been drunk just twice in my life, and
the second time was that afternoon.

I asked Myrtle how she'd ended up with
Wilson. 'I thought he knew something about
breeding,' she replied bitterly, 'but he wasn't
fit to lick my shoe!'

Some time toward midnight, an altercation
broke out between Tomcat and Myrtle.

'Daisy!' screeched Myrtle. 'I'll say it
whenever I want to! Daisy! Dai—'

Making a short deft movement, Tomcat
swiped at her nose with his open paw.

The scene descended into yowling
hysteria, and someone threw a shoe through
the window. I took my hat from the
chandelier and slunk out the cat flap.

All through the summer nights there was music from the parties at my neighbour's house. Every Friday five crates of finest cashmere and merino wool balls of an array of rich colours would arrive – every Monday this same yarn left his back door in flamboyant mountains of fluff. Caterers would fill buffet tables with glistening caviar, roasted quail and turkeys bewitched to dark gold, and fountains of double cream would flow.

By seven o'clock the orchestra would arrive, and the opera of meows and cat-calls would pitch a key higher. Creatures in primary colours and fur combed in strange new ways would break out in dance, and thus the party would truly begin.

One Saturday morning I received an invitation – the honour would be entirely Catsby's, it said, if I would attend his 'little party' that night.

So later I padded, rather ill at ease, among swirls of cats I didn't know. I was on my way to get roaring drunk from sheer embarrassment when someone at my side struck up polite conversation.

'This is an unusual party for me,' I confided in my new acquaintance. 'I haven't even seen the host – this Catsby.'

He looked at me quizzically. 'But I'm Catsby, old sport,' he said, smiling with understanding and reassurance as I begged his pardon.

M uch later I encountered Jordan Baker exiting the library with Mr Catsby. Her eyes were wide with astonishment, and she whispered to me, 'I've just heard the most amazing thing. I swore I wouldn't tell it and here I am tantalizing you. Please come and see me . . .' She was hurrying off as she spoke.

I joined the last of Catsby's guests clustering around him, to apologize for not having known him earlier.

'Don't give it another thought, old sport,' he enjoined me eagerly. 'Good night.' He smiled – and suddenly there seemed a pleasant significance in being among the last to go, as if he had desired it all the time.

I met Jordan in the garden of the Plaza Cattery soon after, and she told me the unbelievable tale. Five years ago, when she and Daisy were home in Louisville, Daisy had had an army officer beau by the name of Jay Catsby. He used to look at Daisy in a way that every young cat wants to be looked at some time, and for a month they were inseparable.

Daisy was disconsolate when he went away to war, but time passed and she was as gay as ever once more. By June 1919 she was engaged to Tomcat, who made arrangements for a wedding with more pomp and circumstance than Louisville had ever known.

But the night before her wedding, Jordan found Daisy lying on her bed, drunk as a monkey and clutching a letter. The pearl collar Tomcat had given her as a wedding gift was lying in her litter tray. She gestured at the collar and said, 'Here, deares', take it and give it back. Tell 'em Daisy's change' her mine!' And she cried and cried.

'I cleaned her up,' Jordan said, 'and next day she married Tomcat without so much as a shiver. From then on I never saw a kitty so mad about her mate.'

'After you came to visit Daisy for dinner,' Jordan continued, 'she came to my basket and asked whom I'd meant when I'd mentioned Catsby. When I described him, she said in a strange voice that it must be the cat she used to know. It was only then that I made the connection between the officer and Catsby.'

'What a strange coincidence,' I mewsed.

'Not at all. Catsby bought his house so that Daisy would be just across the bay.' As I absorbed this, and thought about the green eyes Catsby had been reaching toward that night, Jordan added, 'He wants to know if you'll invite Daisy to your house some afternoon and then let him come over. But Daisy's not to know about it.'

The day agreed upon was pouring with rain. At two o'clock a greenhouse-worth of flowers arrived, as well as a disgruntled cat in a raincoat pushing a lawnmower. When Catsby himself entered, he looked harrowed, and his fur was all mussed from sleeplessness. He curled up miserably and we waited in silence, until finally we heard Daisy's exhilarating cry in the garden: 'Is this absolutely where you live, my dearest one?'

She pranced into the house, stopping short when she saw Catsby. For half a minute there wasn't a sound. Then Daisy said on a clear artificial note: 'I certainly am awfully glad to see you again.' A pause; it endured horribly

I swiftly excused myself, and for half an hour I left them alone. Then – making every possible noise – I re-entered the room. I don't believe they heard a sound. They were sitting at either end of the couch, looking at each other as if some question had been asked. Every vestige of embarrassment was gone, and Daisy's whiskers dripped with tears. But there was a change in Catsby that was simply confounding; a new well-being radiated from him and filled the little room.

'Oh, hello, old sport,' he said ecstatically, as if he hadn't seen me for years.

The next time Catsby had a party, Daisy came with Tomcat. They arrived at twilight, and we strolled out among the sparkling hundreds. 'I've never met so many celebrities!' Daisy whispered.

Daisy and Catsby danced the loxtrot, then sauntered over to my house and perched on the steps, while I remained watchfully in the garden.

But as the night went on, it became clear that apart from the moments she'd spent alone with Catsby, Daisy wasn't having a good time. She was appalled by West Fish, by its raw, new-money air; she saw something awful in the very simplicity she failed to understand.

'She didn't like it,' he said later that night, when it was all over. He was unutterably depressed. 'It's hard to make her understand.'

He wanted nothing less of Daisy than that she should go to Tomcat and say: 'I never loved you.' After she had obliterated four years with that sentence then they could go back to Louisville and be married – just as if it were five years ago.

'I wouldn't ask too much of her,' I ventured. 'You can't repeat the past.'

'Can't repeat the past?' he cried incredulously. 'Why of course you can!'

As obscurely as it had begun, Catsby's party-hosting career was over. Cars would arrive on a Saturday, wait a few minutes and turn sulkily away. He also fired all of his old servants. 'I needed discreet staff,' he explained. 'Daisy often comes over in the afternoons.'

Tomcat was beginning to notice something was amiss with his mate. 'By God,' he frowned at me one day, 'I may be old-fashioned in my ideas, but females run around too much these days to suit me. They meet all kinds of crazy fish.'

On the hottest day of the year, Catsby and I were invited to lunch at the Buchattans'. We ate in the dining room, darkened against the heat, and drank down nervous gaiety with cold milk.

'Who wants to go to town?' demanded Daisy insistently. Catsby's eyes floated toward her. 'Ah,' she cried, 'you look so cool.'

Their eyes met, and they stared together at each other, alone in space. With an effort she glanced down at the table.

'You always look so cool,' she repeated.

She had told him that she loved him, and Tomcat saw. His jaws opened a little, and he looked at Catsby, and then back at Daisy.

'Come on,' Tomcat broke in abruptly, 'we're all going to town. Come on!' He bullishly insisted on driving Catsby's yellow sports car, but Daisy moved away from him and said she was going with Catsby. 'We'll follow in the coupé,' she said.

On the way into the city, Tomcat stopped for gas at Wilson's garage. As we got back into Catsby's car, I saw that in one of the windows of the garage the curtains had twitched, and Myrtle Wilson was looking out. Her eyes, wide with jealous terror, were fixed on Jordan, whom she took to be Tomcat's wife.

We all met at the Plaza Cattery and decided to book a suite and drink milk juleps. We weren't long in the stifling room before Tomcat rounded on Catsby and hissed, 'What kind of a row are you trying to cause in my house anyhow?'

Catsby sprang up and arched his back. 'Your mate doesn't love you! She never loved you!' he cried. 'Daisy, just tell him the truth, and it's all wiped out forever.'

Daisy hesitated. 'I never loved him,' she said, with perceptible reluctance. Suddenly she threw her julep on the carpet. 'Oh, you want too much!' she cried to Catsby. 'I love you now – isn't that enough?' She began to yowl helplessly. 'I did love him once – but I loved you too.'

Tomcat turned to Daisy. 'I'm going to take better care of you from now on.'

'You don't understand,' said Catsby. 'Daisy's leaving you.'

Tomcat opened his eyes wide and shook with mirth.

'I am, though,' said Daisy, with visible effort. But her frightened green eyes told that whatever intentions, whatever courage she had had, were definitely gone.

Tomcat knew he had won. 'You two start on home, Daisy,' he said. 'In Mr Catsby's car. Go on, he won't annoy you. I think he realizes that his presumptuous little flirtation is over.'

Tomcat chattered incessantly on the drive, exulting and laughing, while Jordan and I sat silently. As we approached Wilson's garage we saw a large crowd had formed. 'A wreck?' Tomcat wondered excitedly. 'We'll take a look.'

We entered the garage – and there was Myrtle Wilson's body, covered with a blanket, lying on a worktable. Mr Wilson was keening in a corner. 'She ran out into the road, waving at this yellow car,' a policeman said. 'Auto hit her. Instantly killed.'

We got back into the coupé and raced along through the night. In a little while I heard a low husky sob.

'The God damned coward!' he whimpered. 'He didn't even stop his car.'

Back at the Buchattans', Tomcat and Jordan went inside, while I stayed outside and found Catsby looking up at the house. 'I'm just making sure she's all right, in case he tries any brutality.'

I paused. 'Was Daisy driving, Catsby?'

'Yes,' he said after a moment, 'but of course I'll say I was. She was very nervous when we left Mew York and thought it would steady her to drive . . . It all happened in a minute.'

I left Catsby and looked in the window of the kitchen. Daisy and Tomcat were sitting across the table from one another, his paw on hers. There was an unmistakable air of natural intimacy about the picture, as if they were conspiring together.

It was the following day that Catsby told me he was really James Catz, the son of shiftless, unsuccessful farm cats. He had changed his name as an adolescent, and became just the sort of Jay Catsby an adolescent would be likely to invent. He set out to achieve the glory for which he knew he was destined.

Daisy was the first 'nice' kitty Catsby had ever known, and he thought her and her rich, full life extraordinary. But he knew that under his army uniform he was penniless, a cat without a past, and he couldn't take care of her the way he'd led her to believe.

While Catsby was away, Daisy's letters became more and more despairing. She wanted her life shaped now, immediately, by some force – of love, of money, of practicality – that was close at paw.

That force took shape with the arrival of Tomcat Buchattan.

I left Catsby after breakfast to go to work.
I didn't want to go – I didn't want to leave
him. 'I'll call you up,' I said finally.

'Do, old sport . . . I suppose Daisy'll call
too.' He looked at me anxiously.

'I suppose so.'

We shook paws and I started away. Just
before I reached the hedge I turned around.

'They're a rotten clowder,' I shouted
across the lawn. 'You're worth the whole
damn pounce put together.'

I've always been glad I said that. First he
nodded politely, then he broke into that
radiant, understanding smile.

'Goodbye,' I called. 'I enjoyed breakfast,
Catsby.'

That afternoon, Catsby's chauffeur heard a great splash. He knew that Catsby was sitting by the swimming pool, awaiting a message that Daisy had called. By the time he investigated, it was too late – Catsby was found floating in the pool, drowned. A little way off, the body of his murderer, Mr Wilson, lay in the grass, a bottle of rat poison clutched in his paw.

The funeral took place on a rainy afternoon and was attended only by Catsby's servants and myself. None of his former party guests made an appearance. And when I tried to call the Buchattans' house to tell Daisy, they had gone away, and left no address.

She never even sent a flower.

After Catsby's death the East was haunted for me; so, when autumn came, I decided to come back home.

On my last night, I sprawled out on the beach and looked out across the water, where those green eyes no longer flashed. Catsby believed in those eyes, in that future that year by year recedes before us. It eludes us then, but that's no matter – tomorrow we will run faster, stretch out our paws further . . . And one fine morning –

So we beat on, boats against the current, borne back ceaselessly into the past.

THE END

58

Copyright © 2017 Headline Publishing Group Ltd

The right of Headline Publishing Group Ltd to be identified as the
Author of the Work has been asserted by that company in accordance
with the Copyright, Designs and Patents Act 1988.

First published in 2017 by WILDFIRE
an imprint of HEADLINE PUBLISHING GROUP

Illustrations copyright © Martin Hargreaves

1

Cataloguing in Publication Data is available from the British Library

ISBN 978 1 4722 5034 6

Written by Eliza Garrett

Typeset in Perpetua

Printed and bound in Portugal by Printer Portuguesa

Headline's policy is to use papers that are natural, renewable and
recyclable products and made from wood grown in sustainable
forests. The logging and manufacturing processes are expected to
conform to the environmental regulations of the country of origin.

HEADLINE PUBLISHING GROUP
An Hachette UK Company
Carmelite House
50 Victoria Embankment
London EC4Y 0DZ

www.headline.co.uk
www.hachette.co.uk

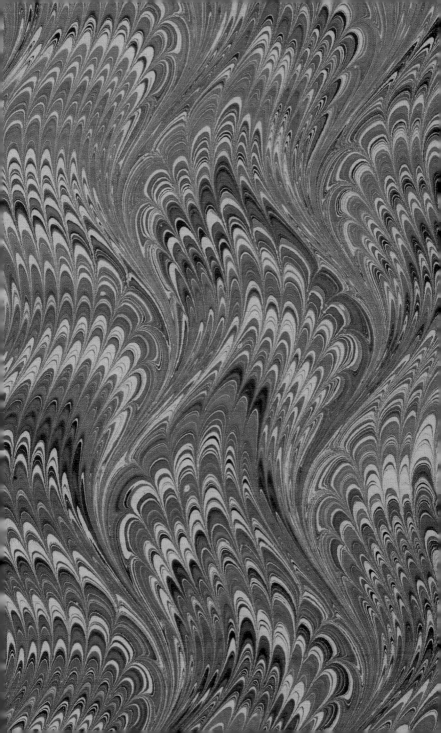